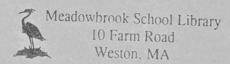

NADIA'S HANDS

by **Karen English**

Illustrated by
Jonathan Weiner

Boyds Mills Press

For Nadia, Sajjad, Maliha, Manar, Mohammed, Dzeneta, and April
—K. E.

To my parents, Joel and Laurie,
for their love, support, and trust
—J. W.

# ❋ Note ❋

Nadia is a Pakistani-American girl. Some of the words in this story are Urdu, the language of Pakistan. Here are the meanings of those words and how to pronounce them:

kabab (kah-BAHB): a dish made of spiced mincemeat grilled over fire.

mehndi (MEHN-dee): a paste made from the leaves of the henna tree. It can be applied to women's hands. When it dries, the paste turns the hands an orange or dark red color. Pakistani women draw elaborate designs with *mehndi* for festive occasions.

shalwar (shahl-WAAR): a loose-fitting, trouser-like form of dress popular among males and females in Pakistan.

kameez (KAH-meez): a long shirt-like upper body dress.

sabr (SAHB-r): This is actually an Arabic word meaning patience, to accept waiting.

For Auntie Laila's wedding, the aunts decided that it was Nadia's turn to be flower girl.

One cousin, who'd been flower girl for the last wedding, said, "I forgot and sprinkled rose petals down just one side of the aisle. Don't make that mistake."

Another cousin, who had been flower girl for Auntie Saleha's wedding, told her, "Oh, I ate too many *kababs* the night before and got sick and had to run to the bathroom right in the middle of walking down the aisle. Take my advice. Stay away from *kababs*."

"Be careful of frozen feet," another cousin added. She had also been a flower girl once. "I got stage fright just as I was about to walk down the aisle. My feet froze."

So many things to remember.

"You know what, Nadia?" Auntie Laila said. She lowered her voice and put her lips close to Nadia's ear. "I have a feeling you're going to be a very good flower girl."

Nadia smiled, relieved.

"I have a special surprise," Auntie Laila added. Nadia waited.

"Auntie Amina's coming Saturday to put the *mehndi* on your hands." Auntie Laila's eyes danced and sparkled. "Just you wait."

Nadia's smile made her face feel stiff. She didn't want the *mehndi*. It would make her hands orange, it wouldn't wash off, and she didn't want to go to school like that on Monday. She was worried.

But on Saturday Nadia forgot her worry and woke up filled with anticipation. The aunties came, one by one, to help with the wedding preparations. One brought the silky, peach-colored *shalwar* and *kameez* Nadia would wear for her duties as flower girl. Another brought tiny gold earrings. Another came to curl Nadia's hair.

Finally, in came Auntie Amina with her bag of *mehndi*.

"Nadia, you go play while Auntie gets everything ready," Mommy told her.

Auntie took from her bag the mixing bowl, the spatula, and the thin wooden stick that looked like a sculptor's tool. She looked over at Nadia. "I'll call you when it's ready, Nadia. It has to sit awhile."

At last, Auntie called Nadia to the kitchen.

"Sit," she said.

Nadia sat.

"Hold out your hands."

Nadia held out her hands and Auntie Amina smeared the *mehndi* all over Nadia's palms. It was cold and pasty and had a funny smell.

"Hmmm," Auntie said mysteriously. With her wooden stick, she began to draw the intricate designs that all the aunties loved. While she did this delicate work, she sang softly to herself a song in Urdu, one that Nadia had heard many times before.

Nadia did not budge. She almost did not breathe. When Auntie was done, Mommy and the other aunts *oohed* and *aahed* at the swirls and the flowers and the stars on Nadia's hands.

Then Auntie Amina drew a small gold ring out of her pocket and smiled a sly smile. "Look what I brought for you for when your hands are ready."

"Thank you," Nadia said, then quickly turned to Mommy. "How long do I have to sit here?"

"For a while."

"What's 'a while'?"

"Be patient, Nadia. Remember *sabr*—patience."

Nadia watched Mommy and the aunts walk out of the room to gaze at the wedding dress—again.

Nadia sat and sat. She sat watching the door, wishing someone would come back through it. She sat watching out the window, wishing there was something interesting to see. Finally, she sat watching the big kitchen clock over the stove. *Tick, tick, tick.*

Uncle Omar came by with a flower delivery. He stopped in the kitchen where Nadia sat, palms up, very still.

"Ah, *mehndi*," he said, and nodded approvingly.

Uncle Abdul Raheem came next. He stopped by the kitchen to peek in the simmering pots on the stove, part of the wedding feast.

"Ah, Nadia," he said, turning around. "You were so quiet and still, I didn't know you were there."

"I'm showing everyone I have *sabr*," she said.

That made Uncle laugh. He went over to her and gazed down at her upraised palms. "Oh, you got your hands done for the wedding. That's nice," he said.

"Yes, Uncle." But really she didn't feel it was so nice.

After a while, a long while, Auntie Amina came and rinsed off the *mehndi*.

Nadia looked down. She had amber hands with deep orange flowers and swirls and stars. Her hands did not look like her hands. They looked as if they belonged to someone else. She didn't want these hands that didn't look like her hands.

Auntie slipped the ring on her finger, and Nadia rubbed its smooth, shiny surface with her thumb.

Now it was time for the wedding. Nadia stood at the beginning of the long, red-carpeted aisle. Everyone in the banquet hall looked back at her. She moved one foot. It wasn't frozen. And, except for the flutter of butterflies, her stomach felt fine. She scooped up a handful of petals from her basket, remembering to toss them first on one side, then the other. She saw a sea of eyes following her. Her feet stayed with the beat in her head. It wasn't so hard. She almost glided down the aisle as she let go of her showers of petals.

But then the bright amber stone in her ring caught the glittering light and Nadia noticed her hands for the first time, it seemed—the swirls and tiny flowers and stars, the bright amber color, the deep orange fingertips. Her heart began to pound at the sight of those hands that she'd have to take to school on Monday—those hands that looked as if they belonged to someone else.

She lost the rhythm then, and brought her foot down so fast that she nearly stumbled. She felt her face grow hot and imagined it red as a pomegranate.

She looked over at the cousins. One was giving her flat, heavy-lidded look. A tiny smile was starting on another one's lips as if she were getting ready to laugh. Behind her hand, the third leaned over and said something to the other two. Then all three turned back to watch Nadia, their eyes three pairs of scrutinizing slits, with smirks hidden behind their solemn expressions.

Nadia's breath came fast. She plucked a few petals
and cast them limply. Then her eyes met Grandma's.
Grandma's eyes were filled with tears but her mouth had
a happy smile. She looked at Mommy and Daddy next.
Their smiles were full of tenderness and the aunts' and
the uncles' smiles were full of affection.

Her feet found the rhythm and she went on—one foot
in front of the other, forgetting her hands as she dipped
into the basket and sprinkled the flower petals first on
one side, then the other, all the way to the end of the
aisle.

After the ceremony, one by one, the aunts came over to admire Nadia's hands and have her twirl around to show off her curls. The uncles came over to lift her chin and smile down at her. Grandma came over and lifted one hand, then the other. "You know what, Nadia?" she whispered. "When I look at your hands, it's as if I'm looking at my past and future at the same time. Did you know that?"

"No, Grandma," Nadia said. What she knew was that her hands made Grandma happy, and Mommy and Daddy and the aunts and uncles. So they made her happy, too.

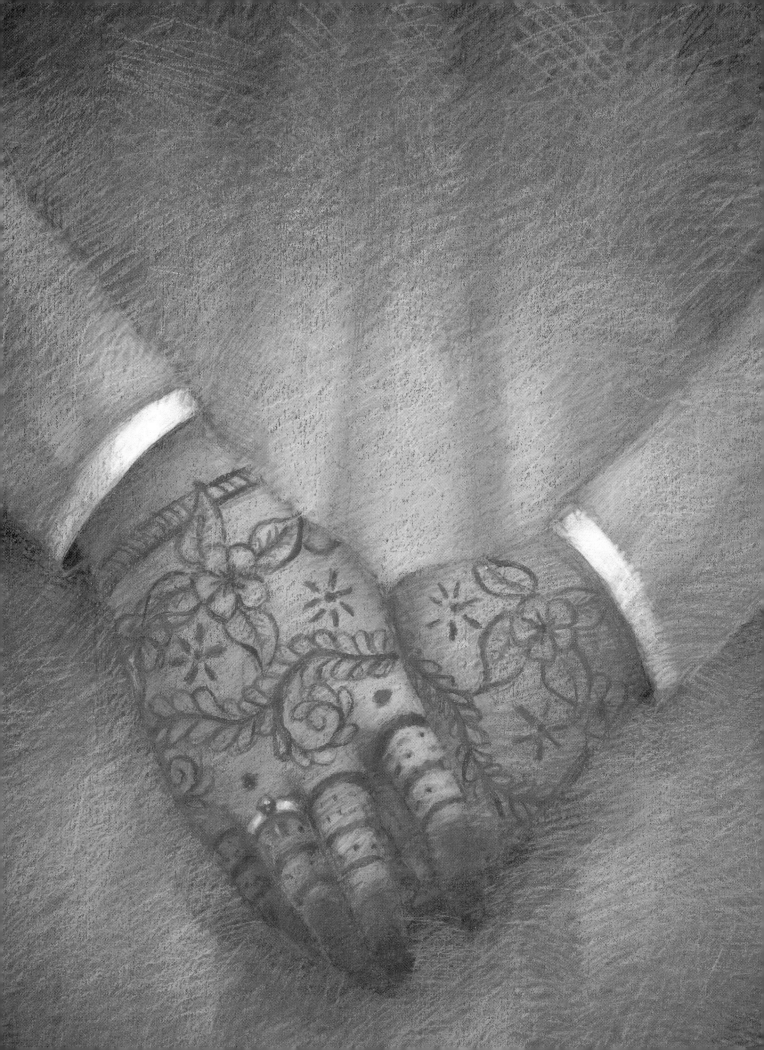

She thought about Monday—at school. Maybe she could show her hands during sharing time. Linda Murakami came with her grandmother's kimono once, and Rashid shared the kinte cloth his mother brought back from her trip to Africa. She would share her hands from Pakistan.

Nadia looked down at her hands. She turned them this way and that. Her hands didn't look as if they belonged to someone else, she decided. They looked as if they belonged to her.

The publisher wishes to thank Javid Aslam of the Consulate General of Pakistan, and Zahra Kahn, editor of the Pakistan Association of Greater Boston Newsletter, for their help in the creation of this book.

Published by Caroline House
Boyds Mills Press, Inc.
A Highlights Company
815 Church Street
Honesdale, Pennsylvania 18431
Printed in China

Publisher Cataloging-in-Publication Data
English, Karen
Nadia's hands / by Karen English ; illustrated by
Jonathan Weiner.— 1st edition.
[32]p. : col. ill. ; cm.
Summary: A Pakistani-American girl takes part
in her aunt's traditional Pakistani wedding.
ISBN 1-56397-667-6
1. Pakistan—Social life and customs—Juvenile fiction. 2. Weddings—
Fiction—Juvenile literature [1. Pakistan—Social life and customs—
Fiction. 2. Weddings—Fiction.] I. Weiner, Jonathan, ill. II. Title.
[E]—dc21   1999   CIP
Library of Congress Catalog Card Number 98-71668

First edition, 1999
Book designed by Tim Gillner
The text of this book is set in 16-point Tiepolo Book.
The illustrations are done in oil pastel.

10 9 8 7 6 5 4 3